# Little Boy Full of Love

River Birch Press

Mesa, Arizona

A Gift to

_____


From


_____

*Little Boy Full of Love* by Robert Masucci

Copyright ©2024 Robert Masucci

All rights reserved. This book is protected under the copyright laws of the United States of America. This book may not be copied or reprinted for commercial gain or profit.

ISBN 978-1-956365-63-4  (print)
ISBN 978-1-956365-64-1  (e-book)

For Worldwide Distribution
Printed in the U.S.A.

River Birch Press
P.O. Box 7341, Mesa, AZ 85216

To my son
whom I love dearly

Robert Oliver Masucci

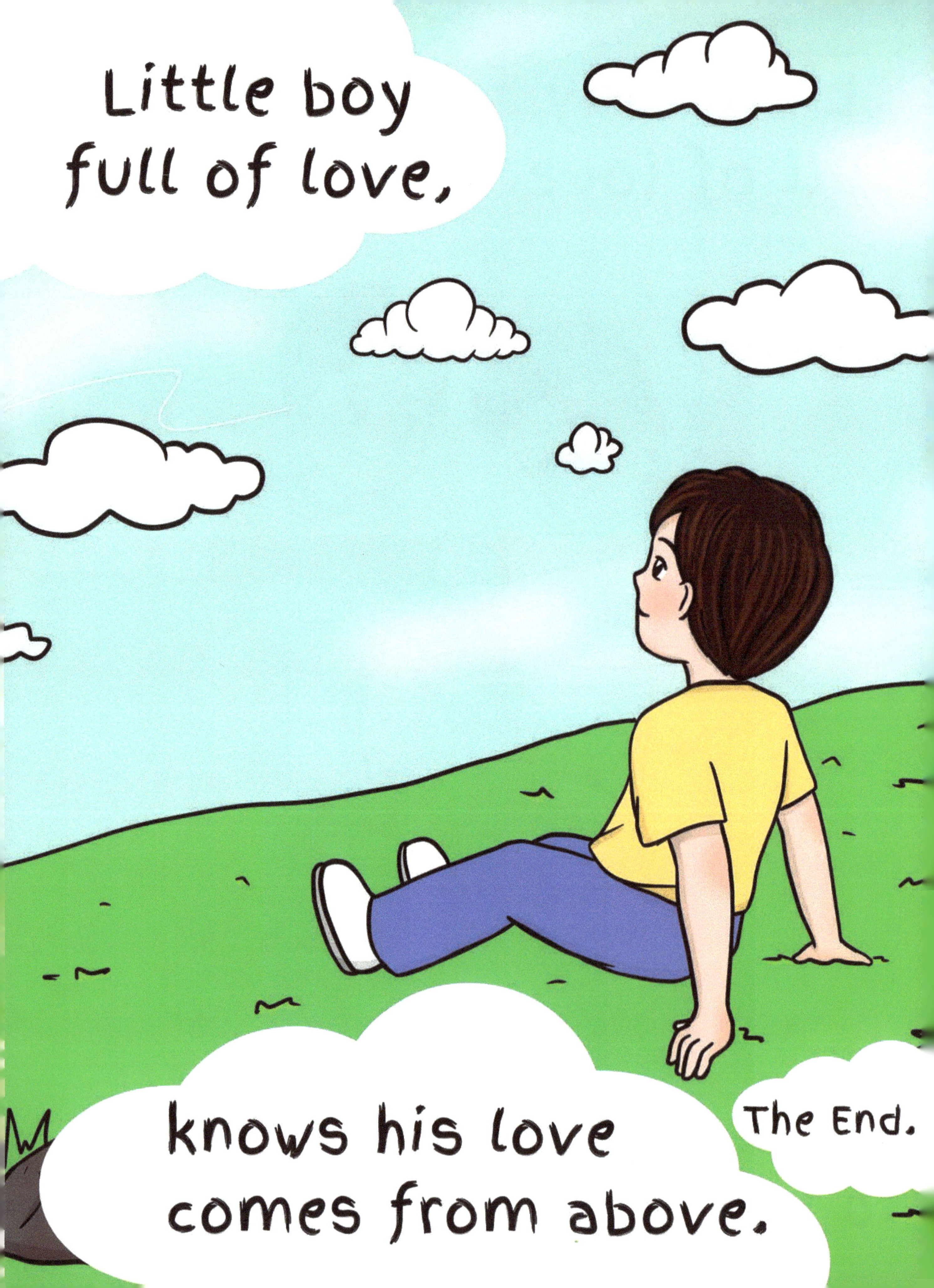
Little boy
full of love,
knows his love
comes from above.
The End.

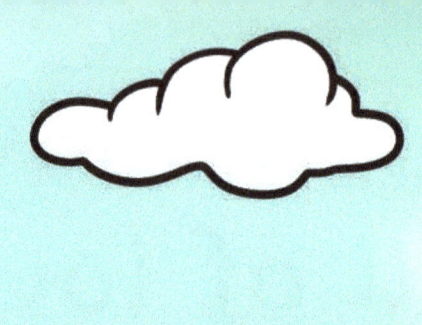

## About the Author

As a father himself, Robert not only was inspired to write a children's book, but he wrote and dedicated this book to his son. Robert saw that although many of the books his wife and he had received as gifts for their son were cute, they lacked wisdom and life lessons. He decided to offer something to parents that they would not only enjoy reading to their children but also be proud to share with them.

This is Robert's first published children's book. He hopes it will become a keepsake for your children and passed down through generations.

Printed in the USA
CPSIA information can be obtained
at www.ICGtesting.com
LVHW060758140124
768912LV00043B/1677